By Deborah Underwood Illustrated by Renata Liwska

Houghton Mifflin Books for Children
Houghton Mifflin Harcourt
Boston New York 2010

For Sarah, with love —D.U.

To my editor Kate, for her support and trust —R.L.

Houghton Mifflin Books for Children is an imprint of
Houghton Mifflin Harcourt Publishing Company.

www.hmhbooks.com

The text of this book is set in Clichee.
The illustrations are drawn with pencil and colored digitally.

Library of Congress Cataloging-in-Publication Data is on file.

ISBN 978-0-547-21567-9

Printed in Singapore
TWP 10 9 8 7 6 5 4 3 2
4500217341

There are many kinds of quiet:

First one awake quiet

Jelly side down quiet

Don't scare the robin quiet

Others telling secrets quiet

Coloring in the lines quiet

Thinking of a good reason you were
drawing on the wall quiet

Hide-and-seek quiet

Last one to get picked up from school quiet

Swimming underwater quiet

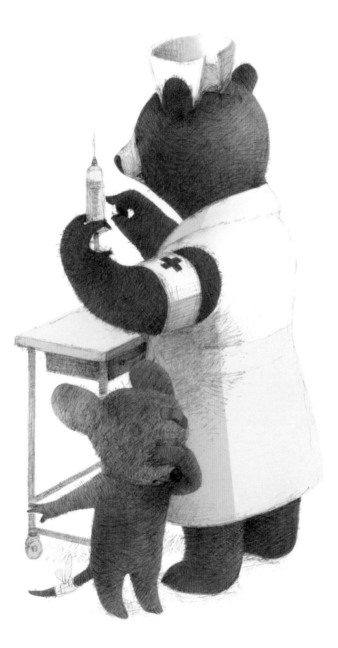

Pretending you're invisible quiet

Lollipop quiet

First look at your new hairstyle quiet

Sleeping sister quiet

Right before you yell "SURPRISE!" quiet

Making a wish quiet

Top of the roller coaster quiet

Best friends don't need to talk quiet

Surprise visit from Aunt Tillie quiet

Do iguanas bite? quiet

Before the concert starts quiet

Trying not to hiccup quiet

First snowfall quiet

Car ride at night quiet

Too many bubbles quiet

Story time quiet

Tucking in Teddy quiet

Bedtime kiss quiet

"What flashlight?" quiet

Sound asleep quiet